HI, I'M TILLY.
WHAT'S YOUR
NAME?

THIS BOOK BELONGS TO:

TILLY TAILS
A DAY AT THE BEACH

WRITTEN BY MEAGHAN V. MOONEY
ILLUSTRATED BY MARLI RENEE

Tilly Tails: A Day at the Beach

Published by Meagnetic Media
www.MeagneticMedia.com

Written and Created by Meaghan V. Mooney
Illustrations and Cover Design by Marli Renee

Library of Congress Control Number: 2020908962

ISBN paperback: 978-1-7350908-0-1
ISBN hardcover: 978-1-7350908-1-8
ISBN ebook: 78-1-7350908-2-5

For more information, visit:
www.TillyTails.com

And connect with Tilly!
@TillyTailsBook

TO DAD

You have given me all the things I need in life and so much more. There is no one more generous, selfless, and thoughtful than you. Thus, showing you the appreciation you deserve has been both simple through emotions, yet challenging through gift. It took thirty-plus years, but I am grateful I finally found the ultimate present to give you in return...
Tilly.

AT THREE YEARS OLD, I TRAVELED SOLO,
TO A DOG SHELTER IN COLORADO.

ONE DAY, I GOT A VISITOR NAMED MEAGHAN.
RIGHT AWAY, I FELT LOVE AND AFFECTION.

SHE KNEW I'D MAKE A GREAT FRIEND,
TO HER DAD IN RHODE ISLAND.

SO, WE LEFT THE SHELTER AND MADE OUR WAY,
IN AN AIRPLANE, ACROSS THE USA.

WHERE DO YOU LIVE? MARK IT ON THE MAP!

RHODE ISLAND

I WAS EXCITED TO MEET TOM, MEAGHAN'S FATHER.
NOW, WE'RE BEST BUDS AND TAKE ADVENTURES TOGETHER.

EVERYDAY, WE EXPLORE. TOM BY FOOT, ME BY PAW.
THEN, WE SHARE STORIES WITH MEAGHAN OF WHAT WE SAW.

"TILLY TAILS" ARE WHAT THOSE TALES HAVE BECOME.
LIKE TODAY'S AT THE BEACH, ARE YOU READY TO COME?!

WHY DO WE SPELL IT "TILLY TAILS" AND NOT "TILLY TALES"?
TURN TO THE LAST PAGE!

TODAY, WE'RE EXPLORING A BIG BEACH NEARBY,
WHERE THERE'S SAND, OCEAN, AND A VIEW OF THE SKY.

STEPPING ONTO THE SAND FEELS SOFT, BUT HOT!
THE SUN SURE IS STRONG AND BEAMING DOWN A LOT.

THAT'S WHY BEACHGOERS SIT UNDER THE SHADE,
WITH COOLERS FILLED WITH FRUIT AND LEMONADE.

THEY ALSO USE SUNBLOCK. LOTS OF SQUIRTS AND SPRAYS,
TO PREVENT PAINFUL SUNBURNS FROM HARMFUL SUN RAYS.

TO STAY SAFE, THEY USE MORE AFTER A SWIM,
THROW ON A SHIRT, AND A HAT WITH A BRIM.

HATS ARE ALSO WHAT THE LIFEGUARDS ON DUTY WEAR,
AS THEY KEEP WATCH FOR HOURS FROM A VERY HIGH CHAIR.

I ASK HIM, "DO YOU HAVE THE BEST VIEW OF THE SEA?"
"WE SURE DO!" HE SAYS, AND INVITES ME UP TO SEE.

I SEE OLDER KIDS SWIMMING, YOUNGER ONES SPLASHING,
AND SURFERS RIDING WAVES THAT ARE CRASHING.

I SEE PEOPLE ON ROCKS WITH FISHING POLES,
AND KIDS IN THE SAND DIGGING HOLES.

21

FROM UP HERE, IT'S CLEAR, THERE'S MUCH TO EXPLORE!
SO, TOM HELPS ME DOWN AND WE WALK TO THE SHORE.

AS WE MOVE CLOSER, TOWARD THE WATER,
THE SAND FEELS FIRM AND THE AIR IS COOLER.

HERE, THERE'S ALSO MORE PEBBLES AND SHELLS,
AND EVEN MERMAID'S PURSES, AS WELL.

LOTS TO COLLECT AND THE BEST SAND, TOO,
TO PLAY IN AND BUILD A CASTLE OR TWO.

THAT'S WHAT THESE KIDS ARE MAKING. THEY HAVE THE RIGHT IDEA.
I ASK, "CAN I DIG A HOLE FOR YOU?" AND THEY ALL SAY, "YEAH!"

WITH ALL FOUR PAWS, I DIG AND DIG,
A SAFE SIZE HOLE, THAT'S NOT TOO BIG.

BUT ALL THIS BURROWING,
IN WET SAND EXPANDING,

AROUND MY BODY,
MADE MY FUR MUDDY!

"HEY!" THEY SAY, "THAT'S OKAY."

"GETTING SANDY AND WET IS PART OF THE FUN!
WE WASH OFF IN THE OCEAN WHEN WE'RE ALL DONE."

RHODE ISLAND'S WATERS CAN FEEL A BIT CHILLY,
BUT THAT'S ONLY AT FIRST, SO I LEAP IN SWIFTLY.

ONCE I'M IN, I BEGIN TO SWIM,
BY BREATHING OUT AND BREATHING IN,

WHILE ALL FOUR LEGS PADDLE AND KICK,
AT A STEADY SPEED, NOT TOO QUICK.

PHEW! EXERCISE SURE MAKES ME HUNGRY,
FOR HEALTHY FOOD TO FUEL MY BODY.

SO, I PADDLE BACK TO WHERE I CAN STAND,
AND SHAKE THE WATER OFF ONTO THE SAND.

...EAT A SNACK, DRINK WATER, AND TOWEL DRY.

WHAT A FUN DAY WE HAD EXPLORING THE OUTDOORS!
HAVE YOU BEEN ON AN ADVENTURE LATELY? WHAT'S YOURS?

WRITE ABOUT YOUR ADVENTURE HERE!

_____

_____

_____

_____

ASK AN ADULT TO TAKE A PHOTO OF YOUR STORY AND POST IT TO SOCIAL MEDIA USING @TILLYTAILSBOOK AND #TILLYTAILS. I CAN'T WAIT TO READ IT! – TILLY

"TILLY *TAILS*" VS "TILLY *TALES*"

The word *tails* in the title of this book is an example of wordplay. Wordplay involves using the meanings of words in clever ways. For example, a *tail* is what a dog wags and *tale* is another word for story. Since Tilly is a dog and the tales are about her, she and Tom thought it would be clever to share "Tilly *Tails*" with Meaghan.

MEAGHAN V. MOONEY

Meaghan Mooney grew up in a small beach town in Rhode Island, where she lives and works today as an Emmy Award winning TV Host and Producer. In June 2020, Meaghan used her storytelling skills and creative talents to publish her first children's book and design products under the same title. Meaghan's also a health and wellness influencer, which is a theme throughout her book that speaks to all ages.

MARLI RENEE

Marli Renee is a California-based artist. She uses art to connect with children in meaningful, vibrant ways. In her free time, she is a plant mom and aspiring diver.

Made in the USA
Middletown, DE
13 October 2020